Mickey's Campout

A LEVEL PRE-1 EARLY READER

By Susan Ring

Illustrated by Loter, Inc.

Disney PRESS

New York

An Imprint of Disney Book Group

DISNEY PRESS

First Edition
Library of Congress Cataloging-in-Publication Data on file
ISBN 978-1-4231-1019-4

Manufactured in Malaysia
For more Disney Press fun, visit www.disneybooks.com

Hi, everybody!

Can you say Meeska, Mooska,

Mickey Mouse?

Let's go to the 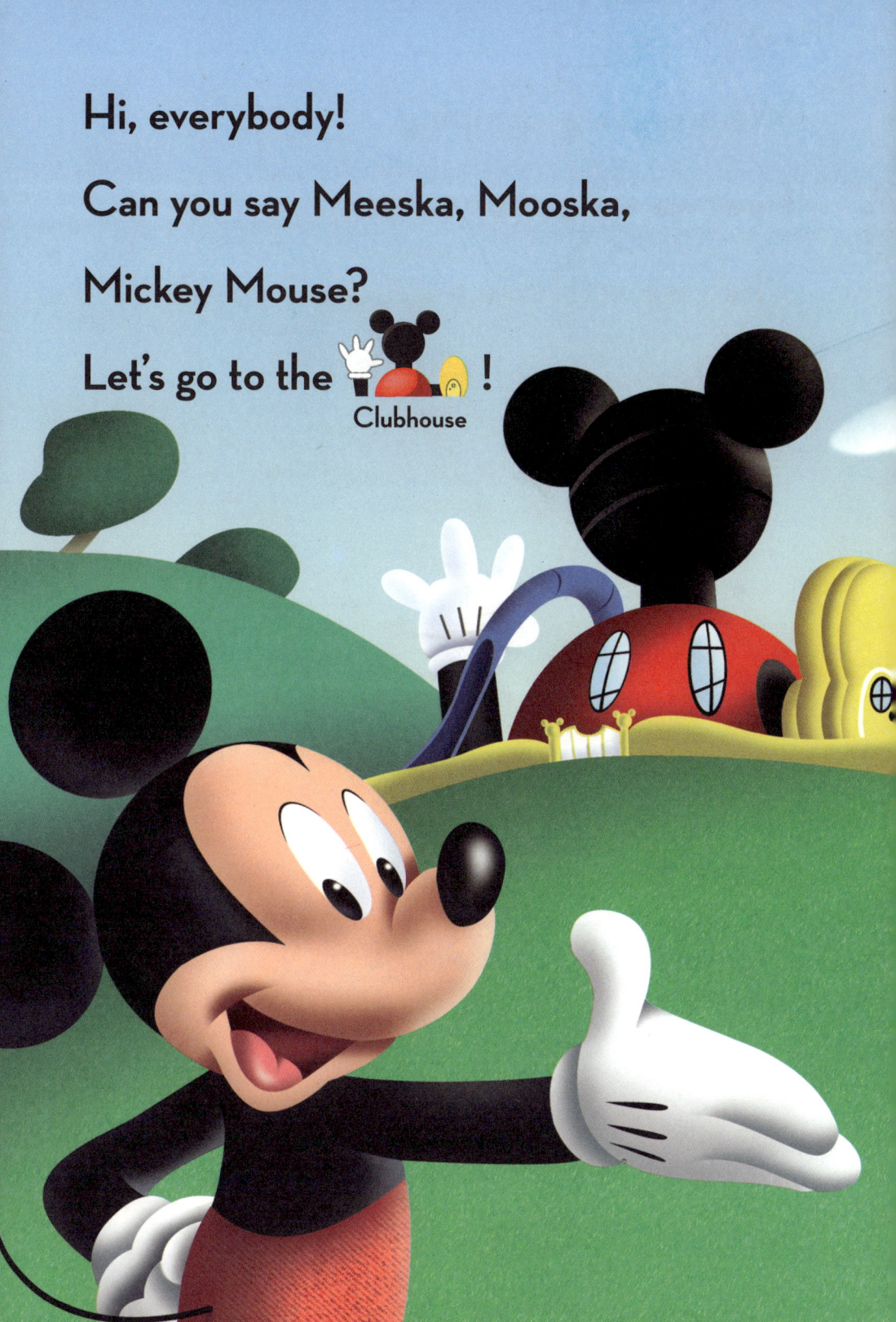 Clubhouse !

We are going camping.

First we will set up a tent.

Then we will have a  .

campfire

Toodles has our Mouseketools.

They are a  , a  , and a  .

pot   woodpecker   Mystery
Mousketool

We are all here!

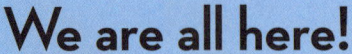 

Minnie, Daisy, Donald, Pluto, Goofy,

and Pete are going camping, too.

Is everybody ready?

Don't forget the tents.

Camping is fun!

Let's set up the first  .

This tent is for [Mickey] and [Donald] .

Uh-oh. The tent is not right.

The [pole] is too long.

How can we make it shorter?

Mickey can't fix the .
tent

Donald can't fix the tent.

Can anyone fix the tent?

We must cut the ⎯⎯ .
pole

Oh, 🔵 !
Toodles

Which tool should we use?

That's right!

The  ! He can cut the _____ .

woodpecker   pole

Now, Donald and Mickey can set up

their ____ .

tent

 and tried to set up their tent.

Daisy Minnie

The tent should look like a big .

balloon

But it is flat like a .

plate

Daisy can't fix the tent.

Minnie can't fix the tent.

Who can fix the tent?

The tent should look like a big 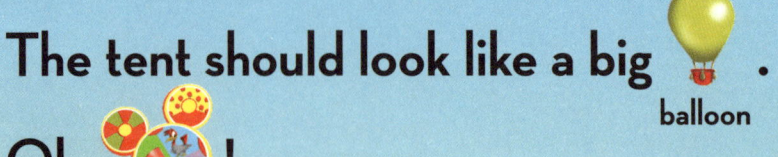 .

balloon

Oh, 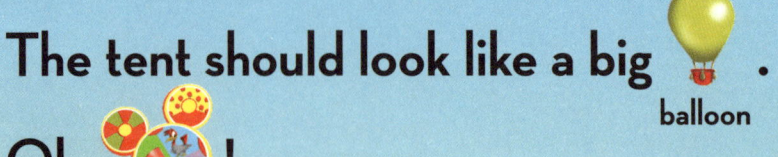 !

Toodles

Which tool should we use?

A 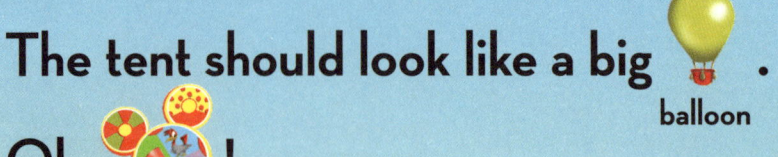 or the 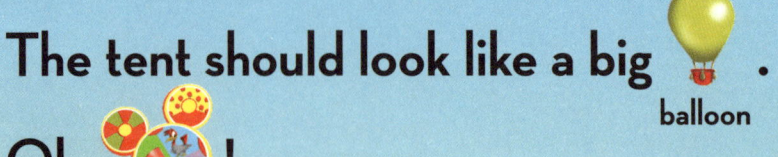 ?

pot   Mystery Mouseketool

A pot is not going to blow air into

the tent.

What other tool can we use?

That's right! The ? is a 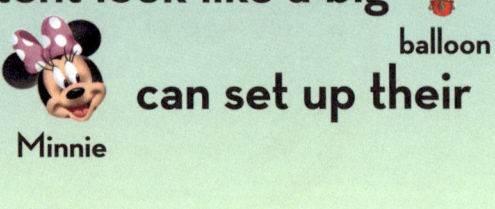 .
Mystery Mouseketool   fan

It will blow air into the tent.

It will make the tent look like a big 🎈 .
balloon

Now, 🦆 and 🐭 can set up their
Daisy   Minnie

tent.

Pete and Goofy were going to set up their tent, but Pete is sleeping on top of it!

What can Goofy do?

Which tool should we use?

Oh, Toodles!

Will the pot do the trick?

Yes! The  is the right tool for Goofy!

pot

Pete wakes up!

Now Goofy and Pete can set up their

tent .

All of the  are up.
tents

Mickey and Donald make a campfire.
campfire

Minnie has a special treat.

It is one of the best things about

camping: marshmallows !
marshmallows